John Keir

AF141059

A Brief Sketch of the Life and Labors of the Late Rev. John Keir

SALZWASSER
VERLAG

John Keir

A Brief Sketch of the Life and Labors of the Late Rev. John Keir

Reprint of the original, first published in 1859.

1st Edition 2022 | ISBN: 978-3-37512-202-7

Verlag (Publisher): Salzwasser Verlag GmbH, Zeilweg 44, 60439 Frankfurt, Deutschland
Vertretungsberechtigt (Authorized to represent): E. Roepke, Zeilweg 44, 60439 Frankfurt, Deutschland
Druck (Print): Books on Demand GmbH, In de Tarpen 42, 22848 Norderstedt, Deutschland

THE LATE REV. JOHN KEIR. D. D.

I. INTRODUCTION.

In proceeding to give an account of the life and labors of this venerable servant of Christ, whose loss the church at large deplores, we may be permitted to express our regret, that he and so many of the fathers of our church have left such scanty records of their early labors and trials. The lives of most ministers is of such a calm and uniform tenor, as to present few materials for biography. It was however very different with those, who first planted the gospel in the forests of this country. Their lives abounded in arduous toils, in spirit stirring incidents, and in abundant success; the record of which would form an interesting addition to religious literature. But with the modesty that characterised them, they, with scarcely more then a single exception, left no written record of their labors and sacrifices. They kept no journals. They neither courted nor expected notoriety for what they had done. They were content to labor and look for no other reward, than the blessing and approval of the great master whom they served. Or if they looked to posterity, it was in the hope, that their works would follow them. This indeed is a record more enduring than the written page, or the marble pillar.— Still we have reason to regret that the facts of their history are so imperfectly known; and justice to their memory, as well as the dictates of the word of God require that, as far as possible, these facts should be preserved. "What we have heard and known, and our fathers have told us, we will not hide them from their children; showing to the generations to come, the praises of the Lord, and his strength, and his wonderful works that he hath done." "Remember the days of old, consider the years of many generations; ask thy father, and he will show thee; thy elders and they will tell thee."

These remarks especially apply to the subject of this memoir. His was a long life of abundant labor, and of cheering success, but he has left no particular record of what he has done. He kept no journal of his early toils, and with the humility of his character, he

erintendence of the Rev. Mr. Ramsay, and afterward of the Rev. Dr.
Muter, then in connection with the Antiburgher Synod. It may be
mentioned that, such was their zeal in attending upon ordinances,
that they at one time walked regularly every Sabbath, between seven and eight miles, to attend upon the preaching of the word.—
Under these ministers Dr. Keir was brought up; in that congregation he first made a profession of religion, and of it he continued a
member as long as he remained in the Old Country.

III. His Student Life.

His parents were in comfortable circumstances, and provided for
him the means of obtaining an education, until he had completed
his college curriculum, which he did at the University of Glasgow.—
Having completed the usual course of literary studies there, he was
admitted to the study of Theology, under the Rev. Archibald Bruce,
of Whitburn, then Professor of Theology to the General Associate
Synod. When about the close of his Theological course, what was
commonly called the New Light Controversy came to an issue.—
This was a controversy regarding the power of the civil Magistrate
in religion. Some portions of the Confession of Faith were inter-
preted as teaching intolerant or persecuting principles; and for several years a controversy agitated both branches of the Secession,
regarding the retention of those portions as part of the Profession
of the Church. It is usual in our day to explain away their force, so
as to make them accord with the principles of toleration, characteristic of the age. We humbly conceive that the Old Light party of
those days, or as Mr. Robertson of Kilmarnock called them, "the
old darkness men," were more honest. They openly advocated the
idea, that the magistrate should employ his "active power" in sup-
pressing heresy, and in advancing the truth. They understood the
language of the Confession of Faith in its full meaning, and regarded "Toleration" of error by the Civil Government, as a national sin.
Among those who took an active part on the Old Light side, was
Professor Bruce, who at length seceded from the Synod. This occur-
red while Dr. Keir was near the close of his course. Though Dr.
Keir retained a veneration for his old Professor, whose talents, learning and character, rendered him worthy of it, yet his sentiments and
feelings ran strongly in favor of the Synod, on the questions at issue.
Indeed, as we shall presently see, he regarded the Synod as behind
the liberal spirit of the age. Dr. Paxton, was on the 30th April,
1807, elected as Professor Bruce's successor, but we believe that Dr.

so much depend on external circumstances, as upon the proper direction of our own minds. I ascribe my lifelessness to the state of my health, which has been poorly for some time past. Indeed, I have never been so well since I came to Mr. Down's, where I still remain. This is perhaps owing to too close confinement, for except the school, which I was obliged to attend, I visited none all last winter . The spring, however, now advancing, "in whose green days reviving sickness lifts her languid head," shall lead me forth "to join the general smile of nature."

I believe that during the last six months, I have made more progress in the study of Divinity, than I did during all my former life. The Bible is now my only text book—all human systems are discarded.—By a close examination of the scriptures my views are greatly changed, so much, indeed, that I am dou tful if I can act consistently in remaining any longer in connexion with the Antiburghers. If they would exercise that candour, towards those who cannot think exactly on some points as they do, which they now profess to exercise, I could have no objection to them; but to profess liberality of sentiment, and at the same time to impose their views upon others, carries a contradiction in the very face of it. It may promote hypocrisy and superstition; but truth must suffer. I have been led into this way of thinking from the conduct of the Synod, which met at Glasgow in August last. They manifested in many respects a very intolerant spirit, especially in the case of Mr. Imrie of Kinkell. He has preached none for some months past in consequence of a recommendation from the Presbytery of Perth. It is greatly feared that he will be deposed at the next meeting of Synod. If this should be the case, it will perhaps do more harm to the Secession Church than the Old Light has done. Toward these brethren the Synod showed an uncommon degree of lenity and forbearance. They were resolved that the separation, if it did take place, would be entirely on their side.

" The Old Lights are very zealous in propagating their doctrines. They have erected the standard of their new party in several congregations already, and are attempting to break the peace and unity of others. We have had Messrs. Aiken and McCrie, preaching in Glasgow, and old Mr. Turnbull has exercised his gifts two or three times. I believe, however, that they will obtain no footing here. That their design is more to gain a party, than to propagate truth, will appear from an anecdote of our late Professor, which I shall now tell you. About two months ago he wrote a letter to Mr. James Aird, telling him that although he might have some scruples about the old Testimony,* yet he and his brethren would overlook these, and take him upon trials immediately, if he would come and join them. He might also expect to get a settlement in one of the principal towns of Scotland, so soon as licensed; which would by no means be the case, if he continued with the Synod's party. How unlike Mr. Bruce!!! To this letter Mr. Aird returned a most complete answer, which mortified him not a little.

Our quondom friend and companion, Mr. Easton, is dead. The Secession Church may mourn the loss, for he was truly an ornament to any society. The comfortable assurance however, that although one event happeneth to the righteous and the wicked, while in this world, yet that the souls of the former are taken away from the evils of time, and made possessors of the glories of eternity, instead of making us sorrow immoderately, as those who have no hope, should turn our sorrow into joy, and our sighs and tears into songs of praise and triumph. You and I, if the scriptures are the word of God, shall meet our dear deceased friend, in due time, without the painful prospect of another separation. In the meantime let us comfort one another with the words of eternal truth. Nothing more is necessary to our deriving consolation from them, but that we believe them. I may also inform you of the death of my sister.   *   *

" Mr. M. has been preaching for some time. He does very well in the pulpit, but I am afraid that he still continues the same unsteady man, when out of it. I do not think that he inclines to undertake a mission to America—at any rate it will be more necessity with him if he do. I think it better not to go at all, than be forced. He had a letter two or three weeks ago from Mr. Bullions,

---

* The immediate cause of the separation was the adoption, by the Synod, of a new Testimony.

tion of the Church, and stirring appeals were coming home, both from the United States and Nova Scotia, to the body to which they belonged, for men to preach the everlasting gospel to the perishing. But there were, at that time, few young men willing to encounter the sacrifices which such a mission involved. His heart was touched, and by intercourse with Mr. Gordon, his desire to preach the gospel to the destitute was increased, so that by the time Mr. Gordon was licensed, about two years before his own licensure, his resolution was taken, and he had pledged himself to his dear friend, that when licensed, he would follow him to the Western wilderness. Thus, he who has the hearts of all men in his hands, was answering the prayers of Dr. McGregor and his associates, by raising up faithful men, to accomplish his purposes of mercy to this country, and putting it into their hearts to come to the help of the Lord against the mighty. It will appear from the above letter, that for a time he hesitated between this country and the United States, where a number of his fellow students, particularly the Rev. Alex. Bullions, had gone. We believe that we are safe in saying, that the matter was finally decided, by his friendship for Mr. Gordon. The latter, on his arrival in P. E. Island, had been called to Princetown and St. Peters. He preferred the call of the latter, and when some of the people of the former place, complained to him of his decision, he replied, that he would get them a better man than himself, alluding to Dr. Keir.— Hence his influence was directed to influence the latter to choose this country as the sphere of his labors, in which he was successful. Having completed his usual term of study, Dr. Keir was duly licensed to preach the gospel, by the Presbytery of Glasgow, about the close of the year 1807, and preached in the various vacancies of the body, till the following summer. At the meeting of Synod in 1808, he formally tendered his services to the supreme court, for the Nova Scotia mission. The Synod was not very anxious to accept his services for the work. There were then many congregations vacant in the church at home, and preachers were very scarce, so that when the question was taken about sending him to Nova Scotia, it was carried in the affirmative, only by a majority of one vote, and even this was only because of his own anxiety to go. It will be thus seen that his coming to this country, was in the true spirit of missionary devotedness, and it may be added, that the sacrifices and trials of missionaries coming to this country, were quite equal to those endured by the majority of modern missionaries. At the time of this decision of Synod, there was an application before them from a congregation just formed in connection with the body at Halifax, and

A BRIEF SKETCH

OF THE

LIFE AND LABORS

OF THE

LATE REV. JOHN KEIR, D. D., S. T.

REPRINTED FROM THE "CHRISTIAN INSTRUCTOR."

PICTOU, N. S.

PRINTED BY E. M. MACDONALD, EASTERN CHRONICLE OFFICE.

1859.

made little reference to what he had done, and in consequence his life can be very imperfectly written. But his labors are written on the face of the country, in the moral wilderness rejoicing and blossoming as the rose. Such facts however as we have been able to glean regarding his life, we shall here record.

II. Parentage and Youth.

The Rev. John Keir was born at Buchlyvie in the parish of Kippon, Stirlingshire, Scotland, on the 2nd February 1780. He was the eldest of the family, which consisted of two sons and a daughter.— The daughter died after reaching maturity, and shortly after her marriage, and the other son has long since preceded him to the eternal world. His parents, whose names were John and Christiana Keir, were very pious people. The district in which they then resided, was one of the earliest in which the Secession had gained a footing, the congregation there being an offshoot of the Rev. Ebenezer Erskine's at Stirling. The people of this parish had been distinguished for their attachment to the Solemn League and Covenant in the bloody days of Lauderdale and Claverhouse, and some of them had suffered and bled in the cause of Scotland's covenated reformation. At the rise of the Secession, when corruption and tyranny were gaining the ascendency in the Church of Scotland, they strongly sympathized with the contendings of the Secession fathers, and cheerfully cast in their lot with them. For ten years, many of them were to be found travelling thirty miles every Sabbath to enjoy the ministrations of Ebenezer Erskine, till their own number, and the increase of preachers in the body, led them, along with their brethren in the neighboring parishes of Balfron, Drymen, and Kilmaronock, to set up a tabernacle for themselves near the centre of the parish of Balfron. They continued to form part of this congregation till the year 1752, when they erected their own place of worship at Buchlyvie.* This congregation it may be mentioned, produced a large number of the early ministers of the Secession. To it belonged, from a very early period, the parents of the subject of this memoir, and so far as Dr. Keir knew, their parents before them; so that by his ancestry he was connected with the Secession from its origin, and at its very fountain head.

When he was about a year old, his parents removed to Baldernock, a few miles distant from Glasgow. Here they became members of the congregation of Duke St., Glasgow, then under the sup-

Keir never attended his prelections. By the appointment of Synod, Presbyteries assigned to Students under their charge, several exercises, and examinations, which were to count as one year's attendence at the Hall.

When he entered upon the study of Theology, his father purchased for him the forms, and other school apparatus belonging to an individual in Glasgow, who was relinquishing teaching for the work of the ministry. Here he taught in the intervals between the sessions of the Theological Hall, during the whole of his Theological curriculum. Here he became acquainted with Mr. Gordon, afterward the Rev. Peter Gordon, of P. E. I., who was then a student of the same body, and who also taught in Glasgow. They for some time lived together and a friendship of the most intimate nature sprung up between them. Of this the following curious epistle may be taken as an expression, as well as affording indications of a sprightliness of character in youth, which many who knew him only in his later years would scarcely suppose him to possess.

Glasgow, 14th October, 1805.

OF ALL BRETHREN THE DEAREST:

Mc Arthur and Keir, servants of Jesus Christ, and about to be called to be apostles, and separated unto the gospel of God,—to thee, Gordon, our dearly beloved brother and fellow laborer, in the vineyard of our common Lord, send greeting:—Grace, mercy and peace, from God, the father, and Christ Jesus, our Lord. We thank God, whom we serve, from our forefathers, with pure conscience, that without ceasing we had remembrance of thee in our prayers, night and day ; greatly desiring to see thee—that we may be filled with joy. And in order to supply thee with the necessaries of life, and to remove all impediments that may stand in the way of thy speedy return to thy place of abode, we send thee forty-two shillings of money, current with the merchant, which by the grace of God we have been enabled to procure for thee. All the saints of God in this place salute thee. Greet the lassie Auld* with a kiss of charity. We salute the brethren which are at Whitburn. Grace. mercy and peace, be with thee, Amen.

Written from Glasgow to brother Gordon by

JOHN MCARTHUR,
JOHN KEIR.

We have a letter before us, to his dearly beloved brother, Gordon, after the latter had come to this country, the most of which we shall transcribe, as it unfolds to some extent Dr. Kier's character during his student life :—

Glasgow, March 10th 1857.

MY DEAR FRIEND.

Your kind letter of the 17th November, I received in due time for which I now return you sincere thanks. It found me in very low spirits, a state of mind, to which I have been of late too much subject. I sometimes wish that I could again enjoy your company as in the days of yore ; but this thought like many others, which pass through my mind is vain ; for our happiness does not

but it gives no encouragement to go to the States. I am expecting a letter every day, either from him or Mr. Bruce, with particular information of the state of religion in that quarter of the world. I have not made up my mind yet, whether I shall go to the States or Nova Scotia. I am rather inclined to the latter. I am determined to give the Presbytery no hopes of going to either, until I be licensed, if ever that be.

"Immediately after the meeting of last General Synod, our Presbytery according to appointment, assigned to every student under their care two discourses, which together with an examination on the system, is to stand for a year at the Hall. They appointed me 2 Cor. x. 18, to the end, for a lecture, and the last clause of verse 20 for a popular sermon. The reason they gave me this passage was, that they understood that I was not sound in the faith upon the doctrine of the atonement, and it was necessary that the Presbytery should be made acquainted with my views on that subject. I delivered the lecture about three months ago, when, as they could find no material difference between my views and their own, it was approved of, and I was ordered to prepare the sermon with all convenient speed. I have it ready, and am to deliver it at next meeting of the Presbytery. In my lecture, I viewed the necessity of the atonement, as arising wholly from the circumstances in which man is placed, and not founded at all upon the divine placability.* I considered the death of Christ merely as the grand means appointed by divine wisdom, for fulfilling that merciful intention, which God has from all eternity entertained toward his fallen creatures. I did not attempt to explain the manner in which the sacrifice of Christ is connected with the forgiveness of sin. It is enough that this is declared by God to be the medium through which our salvation is effected. But I am running on with a subject, in which you are better versed than I am. It gives me pleasure, however, to think that I may write you my sentiments in everything without reserve. I would be very glad that our correspondence should turn upon doctrinal subjects. It would be of great advantage to me in my researches after truth.

"Our Theological society is still existing and in a very flourishing condition. We have got a number of new members since you left us, among whom is Mr. Gilmour, Teacher, opposite the Bank, a gentleman who has exceedingly correct views of the doctrines of the gospel. He and I are generally upon one side of the question. We have very fierce encounters with Mr. Hogg, who always adopts the orthodox side. Mr. Brownlee† is not yet licensed, but he has given in some of his trials, I believe. He will probably go to America. There is a great scarcity of preachers here just now. They cannot get the vacancies all supplied. The Old Light movement has occasioned a number of new ones, and several ministers have been deposed, which makes the demand for preachers very great." * *

"Your brother is just waiting to receive this letter, which prevents me from adding any more. I have not time to read it over. I hope you will excuse any inaccuracies. I shall write you a long letter soon after the meeting of the Synod, with all the news. I hope you will write to me as soon as this comes to hand, with an account of all the news in Nova Scotia, particularly of the state of religion there. I will see you, perhaps, in the course of a year or two.

I remain, Dear Friend.

Yours, sincerely,

JOHN KEIR.

There are several points in this letter worthy of notice. In the first place, we may notice the liberality of his sentiments. He speaks of difficulties about taking license in connection with the Antiburgher Synod. This arose from no scruples regarding the great system of divine truth, as held by that body, for on these his mind

---

† The idea plainly is, that the atonement was not necessary to render God placable. God was always merciful, but the atonement was needed to open a way for the exercise of mercy in consistency with justice.

* Now Dr. Brownlee of New York.

never wavered, but from what he regarded as its intolerant spirit. The narrowness of their views, and the illiberality of their spirit, were exhibited in forms, which to the present age would be almost incredible. For example, [they would suspend a man from church privileges, for hearing sermon in a parish church. A young man of excellent character and promising talents, when nearly ready for license, went to hear sermon from a relative, who had just been ordained in the Established Church. For this he was summoned before the church court, and threatened with suspension if he did not express sorrow for his offence. He offered to express his regret, that he should have done anything that would have given offence to his brethren, but he could not acknowledge anything sinful in what he had done. They refused to accept this, and he left the body, and became a useful minister of another. At the time of which we speak, much of this illiberality had passed away, but so much of it still remained, that it would appear that he scrupled for a time about becoming one of its ministers. This also manifested his strict conscientiousness. It may be mentioned, that the liberal spirit which he thus early imbibed from the study of the word of God, characterized him through life. While none could be more strenuous in maintaining those views of truth, which he had conscientiously adopted, none was more ready to acknowledge excellence, where he found it, in brethren of another name.

Another feature manifested by the above letter, is the independence of his mind. From Dr. Keir's rigid adherence to the old Theology, an impression might have been made on some minds that he would have received his Theological system implicitly from his tutors. Instead of this, it appears plainly from the above letter, that he adopted his views from no human system or human teacher; that he called no man master, and that he drew his knowledge of divine truth directly from the original fountain of wisdom. This appeared, as we shall hereafter notice, in his labors as a teacher of Theology. both from the pulpit and the Professor's desk.

But perhaps the most noticeable feature of the above letter, is the rebuke which it administers to that spirit, not yet extinct in the church, expressively denominated, heresy hunting. If there was one man in our church more than another, in whose soundness in the faith the whole body had confidence, that man was Dr. Keir, and yet it would appear from the above letter, that such was the keen scent for heresy of some would be zealots for the truth, that when a young man, he was suspected as unsound upon a vital point, and had to pass through an investigation, to test the accuracy of his views. It is well, no doubt, to be zealous for the truth, and even jealous for it. But that spirit which is always suspecting error,—is so ready to make a man an offender for a word, and is eagle eyed in detecting some heterodox sentiment lurking under the most innocent expressions,—is most unchristian and injurious. A few months ago, Dr. Keir, in conversing on the subject, informed us that the suspicions arose out of Mr. Imrie's case, referred to in the above letter. This Mr. Imrie was a man of subtle mind, who seemed to delight in exercising his ingenuity in presenting the truths of religion in an unusual manner, or in the form of paradox. This case was for several years before the Synod, and finally he was deposed. But, as Dr. Keir informed us, there was a strong sympathy for him among the students, and from the above letter it appears that he himself had the same feeling, and this led the Presbytery to entertain suspicions of them generally, himself among the rest. In connection with this, he mentioned to us recently, that the Presbytery here in consequence of the case, became suspicious of the orthodoxy of the body at home, and resolved to subject all ministers coming from Scotland, to an examination previous to their being received.

The Theological society mentioned in the above letter, was an association of young men principally students of Theology, for the purpose of mutual progress in their studies. They held regular meetings at which questions in Divinity were discussed, essays were read, and sometimes discourses or plans of discourses delivered and criticised. Of this association, he and Mr. Gordon were members, while they remained in the Old Country, and he ever after recognised it as an important means of advancement in his studies.

IV. DEVOTION TO MISSIONARY WORK, AND APPOINTMENT TO NOVA SCOTIA.

But his intimacy with Mr. Gordon was especially interesting, from its connection with his decision to come to this country. The latter, when a working weaver, had been so touched by one of Dr. Mc Gregor's appeals, setting forth the spiritual destitution of this country, that he resolved to devote himself to study for the work of the ministry, with a view to coming out as a missionary. During the whole course of his studies, he kept this object steadily in view,— and whether his intercourse with Dr. Keir, was the means of *originating* in the mind of the latter, the desire to devote himself to the same work or not, it had at least the effect of strengthening and confirming it. The Missionary work was then occupying the atten-

the Synod sent him out with a special view to that place, giving him liberty to return in two years, if he did not like the country, the expences of his passage home to be paid.

V. FROM HIS APPOINTMENT TO NOVA SCOTIA TILL HIS ORDINATION.

Having thus been duly accepted as a Missionary, he immediately prepared to set out for his destination. Three weeks previous to his departure, he was married to Mary, only daughter of James and Amelia Burnet, persons distinguished for their early and deep piety, and respectable members of Dr. Thomson's congregation in Glasgow, in connexion with the Relief Synod. This union of Secession and Relief was as happy in a domestic point of view, as has the larger union of the same name been in an Ecclesiastical. For the long period of fifty years they have travelled the journey of life together, unitedly bearing its burdens and sharing its joys—"as heirs together of the grace of life." "Lovely and pleasant were they in their lives," and in their deaths they cannot be long divided. It may be here mentioned that during his student life, he enjoyed considerable friendly intercourse with ministers and students of the Relief Synod, and acquired a high esteem for that body. He rejoiced therefore greatly at the steps taken for union between it and the Secession, and when the union did take place, his remark was, that it should have taken place long before. We may also mention that by his marriage he became in right of his wife a Burgess of the city of Glasgow, though had he found it necessary to trade within the bounds of the city, his principles as an Antibugher would have prevented him taking the oath then required of such.*

On the last Sabbath previous to his departure, he proclaimed the gospel of salvation in Greenock, and on the one previous, in Paisley, where a liberal contribution was handed to him to defray the expenses of his mission. In September he set sail from his native land for Pictou, where he safely arrived, and where he was received with great joy by the brethren. The Presbytery were at that time anxious about Prince Edward Island, particulary in consequence of the dis-

---

* It may be necessary to explain, that the Burgesses of certain cities in Britain, have gone the right to do business within certain limits. "The freedom of the city" sometimes presented to men of eminence is the conveyance to them of this privilege. Ridiculous as the idea may seem of giving to such warriors as Lord Clyde or such statesmen as Lord John Russel, the right of dealing in tea or tobacco in the salt market of Glasgow, yet it is considered a compliment, which is received with all due respect. An oath which was required of Burgesses in certain cities of Scotland, produced the division of the Secession into Burghers and Antiburghers, the latter denying the lawfulness of the oath.

appointments the people there had experienced. About eighteen years had elapsed since Dr. McGregor had first preached the gospel in Princetown, and with the exception of a short time, that Mr. Urquhart had laboured among them, they had received only occasional supply of sermon, and had suffered the miseries of hope deferred. In the year 1799 the Synod in Scotland had appointed the Rev Francis Pringle to that place, but coming out by way of New York, the Presbytery there detained him. In the year 1803 Dr. McCulloch was appointed to P. E. Island, but he arrived too late in the fall to get a passage over, and remained in Picton all winter. A party from the former place arrived in Picton to take him over, on the very day of his induction at the latter. Mr. Gordon had been sent to the Island two years previously, but his health was now failing, and it was already seen that he was not to be spared long to labor in the Lord's vineyard on earth. Under these circumstances the Presbytery considered the circumstances of the Island so pressing, that, notwithstanding the application from Halifax, they sent him to the former place for the winter. This decision accorded with his own views, and the appointment as bringing him into close association with his old friend, Mr. Gordon, was particularly agreeable to his feelings.— He and Mrs. Keir accordingly removed to P. E. Island that fall, where he took up his abode at Princetown, lodging for the winter in the house of Mr. John Thomson, one of the elders, near where the present church now stands.

During the most of that winter he preached at Princetown and the adjacent settlements, but he also preached at St. Peters by exchange with Mr. Gordon. The latter came to Princetown in April following, though in a state of great feebleness, to dispense Baptism to the people, while Dr. Keir supplied his place. On his way home Mr. Gordon died at Covehead. Dr. Keir then, we believe, also gave some supply to St. Peters. In spring he returned to the mainland, and during that summer (1809) he supplied Halifax and Merigomish. In the meantime calls came out both from St. Peters and Princetown, the call of the latter being dated 19th June 1809. The people of Halifax and Merigomish also prepared to call him, but the Presbytery in consequence of the state of the Island by the death of Mr. Gordon, were anxious for him to go there, and in his own opinion the finger of Providence pointed out that duty called him thither. In these circumstances the calls from these places were not prosecuted. The people of Halifax were so disappointed that they threatened to join another body.

We have conversed with several persons who recollect him at this period of his life, and it is interesting to look back upon the impressions formed of him then, and compare them with what he showed himself afterward. As to his preaching, it was not of the style, which might be denominated popular, but by the judicious it was relished for its full and clear exhibitions of divine truth. But the most curious fact is that he was regarded, and that by persons having had good opportunities of judging, as disposed to indolence, and by others as rather vain. We could scarcely have imagined any thing more opposite to the tenor of his whole subsequent career. Nothing in his after life seemed more to distinguish him than his laborious and self-denying diligence in duty, and the unfeignrd humility of his character. The impressions formed of him might have been well founded at that time, but if they were, his subsequent life reflects all the more honor upon that divine grace, by which he was enabled so entirely to overcome the tendencies of his natural temperament.

The Presbytery, with whom at that time rested the decision in cases of competing calls, having, in accordance with his own inclination, decided in favor of Princetown, he proceeded thither that season, and there finally took up his abode. But in consequence of what he considered the disorganized state of the congregation, and in order that he might have time to become better acquainted with the people, before dispensing church privileges to them, he requested the Presbytery that his ordination might be deferred till the following season, and that he might be allowed in the meantime to preach to the people as a licentiate. This was agreed to and his ordination accordingly did not take place till June 1810.

Accordingly at that time, the Presbytery proceeded to Princetown for his ordination. The members present were, Dr. McGregor, the Rev. Duncan Ross, Dr. McCulloch and the late Mr. Mitchell of River John. They arrived by way of Bedeque late in the week. Dr. McGregor preached on Saturday from Phil. 3. 8,—"I count all things but loss for the excellency of Christ Jesus my Lord." But the ordination did not take place till the following day, (Sabbath.) An ordination was then an event entirely new in that part of the Island, and excited great interest. There were many doubtless who rejoiced in the event, as realizing their long disappointed expectations, of having the ordinances of religion regularly dispensed among them. But the novelty of the event excited the curiosity of many others. So that the whole population not only of Princetown, but of New London, Bedeque and the west side of Richmond Bay, able to attend, assembled on the occasion. The audience for those days, when population was sparse, was considered immense. The old church would not hold half of the congregation. A platform was accordingly erected outside the church but close by it on which the ordination took place. Part of the audience remained seated in the church within sight and hearing, while the rest were assembled outside.— Dr. McCulloch preached from Acts 17. 3—10, "He hath appointed a day in which he will judge the world in righteousness by that man whom he hath ordained," narrated the steps, put the questions of the formula and offered up the ordination prayer. Mr. Ross gave the charge to the people, and we believe, also to the minister, and Mr. Mitchell concluded the services by a sermon from Acts 13. 26, "Unto you is the word of this salvation sent." But considerable disappointment was felt by the people, that they were not hearing the voice of Dr. McGregor, whom they regarded as the father of the congregation, and to whom many of them individually looked as their spiritual father. As one brother after another occupied the stand, there were whisperings, "will it be him next," and as the services were concluding without his taking any part, their disappointment almost amounted to vexation, but a complete revulsion took place, when after the benediction it was announced that in ten minutes Dr. McGregor would preach in Gaelic. The people of Princetown were originally from Cantyre, in Argyleshire, and the old people mostly spoke Gaelic, so that they eagerly crowded around him to hear the gospel in their native tongue, and such was their interest in it, increased by the revulsion of feeling affecting from their former disappointment, that he had been speaking but a few minutes when the whole congregation were bathed in tears. Altogether the day was one of deep and hallowed interest, and yet has a place in the fondest recollections of the few now surviving of those present, while the young have heard of it traditionally from their parents as a day long to be remembered.

But "when the sons of God came to present themselves before the Lord, Satan also came with them;" and so it seemed to be on the present occasion. There was a man present, who was an infidel and a bold blasphemer. He had considerable skill in sketching, and drew a caricature of the whole proceedings. He pictured Dr. McGregor in one of his postures of greatest earnestness, and words coming out of his mouth, which were a profane caricature of his text, while some of the leading persons of the congregation were represented with mouths open, or in other ridiculous postures. As a caricature it was clever, and was afterward freely circulated. The author was at that time a man of influence—had a fine establishment of Mills—and for a time made considerable money, but he came to poverty, and died in Charlottetown in great wretchedness.

VI. Pastoral Labors.

To understand the nature of the work upon which Dr. Keir now entered, we must take a view of the extent of the congregation, the physical state of the country and the religious condition of the people at the time. Not only did his congregation include Princetown, but it embraced in addition, New London, the few families then residing at Cavendish, Bedeque, and the west side of Richmond Bay, including Lots sixteen and fourteen, what now embraces five congregations, and what will soon be six. "I find" said the Dr. "at his jubilee, that the call was subscribed by sixty-four persons, embracing nearly all the heads of families in Princetown Royalty, New London, Bedeque, and the west side of Richmond Bay. Of these sixty-four persons whose names are to the call, only fourteen remain alive unto this day." Yet for ten years Dr. Keir diligently and faithfully discharged all the duties of the pastoral office over this widely scattered field. He preached at Princetown one half of this time, while the other half was divided among the other settlements mentioned. But his labors were not confined to preaching the gospel. He regularly visited all the families of this scattered charge and regularly held diets of examination in every section.

To appreciate fully the toil which this involved, we must remember the position of the congregation and the physical state of the country. A large bay six miles across, separated between the principal sections, requiring either to be crossed in boats, or rendering necessary a circuit of twenty, or to some parts thirty miles, while smaller creeks and rivers divided other sections, and rendered intercourse between them difficult and fatiguing. Besides, there were scarcely any roads worthy of the name. The most of the travelling was along the shore, and much of it had to be performed on foot.— "There was no broad road" says the Rev. R. S. Patterson "upon which you could comfortably drive in your neat carriage. The best mode of travelling, open to your choice, was riding on horseback; and perhaps the roads might be such as not to admit of this, and the journey must be performed on foot. The wintry storm and the cold northern blast must often be encountered, without the defences which our Buffalo and seal fur coverings now afford us. And although the wearied guest received a cordial welcome, yet his accommodations were anything but comfortable. A hard couch, scantily covered, but ill defending him from the cold, was often his lot. But neither difficulty, nor even danger, to which he was sometimes exposed, could deter him from the faithful performance of the duties of his pastor ate. You might depend upon finding him at his post at the appoint-ed time. For punctuality, that quality so necessary in every one, but more particularly in public characters, he was remarkable."—When we consider the local extent of his congregation; the difficulty of travelling between the different sections of it, and the backward state of the country at the time, we believe that no minister in our church, since the days of Dr. McGregor, has endured more of physi-cal toil in the preaching of the gospel than Dr. Keir. In fact, what Dr. McGregor was in Pictou and adjacent districts, Dr. Keir was in the Island, particularly in the western part of it. Indeed these two men closely resembled one another. They had a similar work to perform and they performed it in the same spirit of faith and zeal.

We may add that the circumstances in which Dr. Keir was placed called for the same self-denial. Like most, if not all the early ministers of our church, he had to suffer from an inadequate stipend imperfectly and irregularly paid. Even now ministers and minis-ters' families are often under the necessity of exercising consider-able ingenuity to prevent embarrassment in their worldly circum-stances But we need not say that this was much more the case with the fathers of the church. Their households often exhibited ex-amples of privations, patiently endured, of which the world knew no-thing. With an increasing family, Dr. Keir had his full share of these. But none ever heard him complain. He patiently endured for the sake of his flock, seeking not theirs but them. And we deem it worthy of special mention, that he never relaxed in the discharge of any of his ministerial duties, in consequence of the inadequacy of support. It has too often been the case that ministers have made the inadequacy of their support an excuse for neglecting some of the duties of their office—either giving up visiting and catechising alto-gether, or giving little attention to the work of preparation for the pul-pit. They have turned to other employments, making the work of the ministry a secondary matter, and the result has been to increase the evil complained of—to render the support still more inade-quate; and often to leave a congregation to spiritual barrenness, and perhaps to send leanness to the minister's own soul. To the temp-tation to relax his diligence in the work to which he had devoted himself, by turning aside to other employments, we are happy to say, that Dr. Keir never gave way. He did indeed, as most of the fathers of the church felt it necessary to do, cultivate a small piece of land to aid in the support of his family, but he did not give his attention to the business of farming, in such a way as to divert his attention from the work of the ministry. This he felt to be his great business, to this he had devoted himself—the vows of God were upon him—and "with his might" he attended to each of its duties. He "gave attendance to reading" as he had opportunity, he wrote out his sermons carefully, and even when most pressed in his worldly circumstances, he regularly visited and catechised his whole congregation, even when its limits were most extensive. And he found in his experience that the name of him whom he served was, *Jehovah Jireh*, "The Lord will provide." Faithfully attending to his ministerial work he found the fulfilment of the divine promise, "Thy bread shall be given thee, thy water shall be sure." He and his family were always provided for. If he ever was in debt, it was but to a limited extent, and never for such a length of time, as to cause any serious embarrassment.

Such indefatigable labor and such disinterested self-denial, accompanied, as from his character we know it must have been, with earnest prayer for the divine blessing, was attended with success. We may remark that the trials through which he was called to pass in the early years of his ministry, had a beneficial effect upon his own mind. Those who are old enough to remember him when he first came to this country and could compare him with what he was a few years after, tell that they could not but remark a deepened humility, a growing meekness, and a ripened spirituality, showing that his path like that of the just was shining more and more unto the perfect day, and that "all things work together for good to them that love God."— And the fruit appeared in his congregation. When he settled among them there were doubtless a number of pious people in all the sections of it, but from their circumstances for many years previously, there must have been general ignorance in religion and indifference to spiritual things. The people of Princetown had settled there, some of them as early as the year 1771, and until Dr. McGregor visited them in 1791, they had scarcely ever heard a sermon. When he first preached among them, there were persons nineteen years of age present, who had never heard a sermon. From that date till the time of Dr. Keir's settlement, a period of nearly twenty years, with the exception of the time of Mr. Urquhart's residence among them, all the supply of preaching they had was from visits of Dr. McGregor and other ministers, scarcely exceeding three or four Sabbaths in the year. Under these circumstances we need not be surprised that much ignorance and spiritual deadness prevailed. The adjacent settlements were not in a more favorable condition. The Rev. Mr. Urquhart had indeed been about two years laboring among them, and had established church order. But he left them in a somewhat

(17)

divided state, and their knowledge of Church order may be judged of by an incident, which took place shortly before Dr. Keir's settlement, which we have heard related by those who witnessed it, of whom some are still living. A member of the church had been guilty of something of which the elders felt it their duty to take cognizance. After due deliberation they resolved, that he should be "put out of the church." Accordingly on the first Sabbath after, on which there was preaching, on his entering the church, one of the Elders sprang from his seat, and beckoned to a brother Elder to come to his assistance, when both proceeded to the spot where the unfortunate sinner was, and seizing him by the collar, they dragged him to the door, and then hurled him as far from the sacred precincts of the building as their united strength enabled them to do.— We are afraid that such rigid discipline was ineffectual in subduing the refractory spirit of the offender, for while the Elders stood guarding the sacred portals, he went away muttering, that they might turn him out of the church on earth, but they could not turn him out of the church in heaven.

We mention these things to show the state of matters at Princetown, when Dr. Keir settled there, that his success may be appreciated. He did not come to a well trained congregation, he had to organize and train it. He did not come to a people well versed in religious knowledge and regular in their religious habits. There were indeed, as we have said, a number of pious persons among them, but the majority he had to train both in religious knowledge and christian duties. But the success of his labors soon appeared. The people generally grew in religious knowledge—the careless and indifferent were aroused—and souls were added to the Lord. The effect of his labors will appear in the progress of his congregation, to which we shall presently advert. But in reference to individuals we may say, that many trace their first serious impressions to his ministrations, and many still living, and many now in glory, could point to him as their spiritual parent. The number of such the great day will disclose, but we have evidence sufficient to satisfy every candid mind, that he will be among the number of those, who "turn many to righteousness, who shall shine as the stars for ever and ever."

Could the history of such individual cases, of men brought to the knowledge of the truth through his instrumentality, be recorded, we believe that there would be abundance of material for an interesting narrative. We will state one incident of the kind, which he mentioned to us the last time we were in his company. When he was finishing the inside of his house, he could scarcely get a carpenter any where to do the work. There was one on the Island, an Englishman, a good workman, but very much given to liquor. Besides, it being the time of the last American war, he had just enlisted in a company, that had been raised by a Captain McDonald from Canada, to serve in that Province against the Americans. They were however unable to get off the island that fall, and they were therefore detained in Charlottetown all winter. There was however no way of obtaining the services of this man, but by having him arrested for debt. Dr. Keir accordingly, induced an individual who had a claim against him, to take out a writ and have him lodged in jail. The Captain was dreadfully enraged, but his wrath was disregarded. Dr. Keir became security for the man and took him out of jail, on condition of his doing the work required in the Dr's house.— The man accordingly came to Princetown, and worked for Dr. Keir most of the winter, lodging in his house. The Dr. embraced the opportunity of dealing faithfully, yet kindly and affectionately with him about the life he was leading, and his spiritual interests, and persevered in his exhortations as long as the man was with him.— The result was an outward reformation. The individual abandoned drinking, and its concomitant vices, and became at least, more thoughtful. There did not at first appear evidence of any more decided change of heart. But the seed sown, afterward bore fruit under very interesting circumstances. In the following spring, he went with his company to Canada, where he served during the remainder of the war. On one occasion, when under fire, another man belonging to the Island, asked him to change places with him. He agreed, but they had scarcely done so, till the other man was shot dead. This event made such a deep impression upon his mind, that in connection with Dr. Keir's exhortations, it led to a thorough change. He returned to P. E. Island at the peace, and has since led a consistent life. For a number of years, he has been a respected Elder in one of our congregations there. We trust that should this meet his eye, he will forgive our reference to his case.

VII. MISSIONARY LABORS.

Extensive as were the bounds of Dr. Keir's congregation, his labors were not confined to it. For two years after he commenced his labors at Princetown, he was the only Presbyterian minister on the Island, and the only Protestant ministers there of any denomination were old Mr. Desbrisay of the chapel church, and one or two others so that there was much of the Island in a state of entire spiritual destitution. In particular, there was the congregation of St. Peters, (embracing not only that settlement, but the neighboring settlements of Covehead, Bay Fortune and East Point), left vacant by the death of Mr. Gordon. The Presbytery being able to afford it but very scanty supply of preaching, he supplied them while they were without a minister, as regularly and as frequently as he could, consistently with his duty to his more immediate charge. About the year 1811 the Rev. Mr. Pidgeon, who had originally been an English Independent, and who had been sent out as a missionary by the London Missionary Society, having applied to the Presbytery, was received as a minister in connexion with the body, and was in the following spring inducted as a minister of St. Peters. But in a few years circumstances rendered it advisable that a dissolution of the pastoral relations should take place, and they were again left vacant. But these were not the only places beyond the bounds of his congregation, to which Dr. Keir directed his missionary labors. He felt deeply for the settlements in almost entire destitution of the word of life, his soul yearned over so many immortals, wandering as sheep wanting a shepherd, and perishing for lack of knowledge, and he spared no labor to visit them. Among the places where he thus preached, may be mentioned Tryon, the West River,* Murray Harbor, Georgetown and Belfast. The Rev. Mr. McKay of the latter place informed the writer, that Dr Keir preached the first sermon ever preached in the latter place, the place of meeting being a saw mill at Point Prim. In fact there is not one of the old Presbyterian congregations on the Island, whether in connexion with the Scottish Establishment, the Free Church or the Presbyterian Church of Nova Scotia, which did not to some extent enjoy his missionary labors, or experience his fostering care in its infancy. In the most of them Dr. McGregor had planted, but he watered, and in some instances reaped the first, but in others he both planted and watered while others have reaped. "Herein is that saying true, one soweth and another reapeth." "That both he that soweth and he that reapeth may rejoice together."

These missionary labors involved much toil and privation. In scarcely any part of the Island was there a road better than a mere footpath through the woods. The greater part of the trave'''' ''' ''' along shore, involving much diffi''''' '' ''''' ' ' '' '''' '''' '' ' '' ' '' ' ' ' '

Often had he to travel considerable distances on foot. The creeks sometimes required him to make a long circuit to go round their head, or had to be crossed sometimes in canoes, sometimes on horseback, when the water would be well up the horse's sides, and we have heard him tell of crossing a stream in the neighborhood of Belfast in the following curious mode. It was too deep to be waded, and there was neither boat nor canoe in the neighborhood. The man in company with him was a good swimmer, but Dr. Keir could not swim at all. In these circumstances, the only plan they could devise to gain the other side was to tie the clothes of both in a bundle, and his companion to swim over with them on his head, and then return to assist Dr. Keir across. This was accordingly done as they proceeded on their way. In these journeys he was not only for days but for weeks from home, and often exposed to piercing cold and wintry storm, with very inadequate protection against their inclemency, and often partaking only of the homely fare and the rude accommodation afforded by the hut of the new settler. But no murmur escaped his lips. He also found the people in many instances very ignorant and careless. We have heard him tell of there being such talking when he began preaching, even after he had spoken to them to be silent, that he had to read the Psalm at the top of his voice to drown their clamour.

His missionary labors however, were not confined to Prince Edward Island. After the death of Mr. Urquhart he visited Miramichi, and preached at different places along the river. He preached at the house of Mr. Henderson, with whom he lodged, at Douglastown, where there was an old church, in the Court House at Newcastle, up at the forks of the river, and at Burnt Church. He also visited among the people, but found them so ignorant in religious matters, that he could not consicentiously dispense to them the sacraments.— As a specimen of this he mentioned to us the following incident.— One man having applied to him on the road to baptize his child, he told him that he must have some conversation with him first. On their way the Dr. happened to ask him who baptized his last child. He replied " the minister, an old woman." "How is that," the Dr. asked. The man replied "The child was very sick, and we sent down the river for the minister, but he was not to be had, and as the child was very sick, the old woman baptized it." The Dr. pressed him to come into Mr. Henderson's house, where he was lodging, that he might converse farther with him. "No," said the man at last, "I will not come in, but if you will baptize my child, I will give you thirty shillings, and if you wont take that I must do without." On

his way down to the place from which he sailed, he and his compan
ions were nearly plunged into the river. Their craft was a species of
canoe called a Laplander, very long and very sharp, made out
of a single tree, and so tender, that a keg which was at one end hap-
pening to roll to one side, was sufficient to destroy its equilibrium,
and in connexion with some carelessness or unskilfulness on the part
of one of the men, almost capsized it. One man was thrown into the river, and they were with some difficulty saved by the skill
of the person in command.

We believe that he afterwards visited Miramichi and some other
parts of New Brunswick. He mentioned to us that on one occasion
he left Miramichi in a gale of wind. But it was right aft of them,
and though the storm was such as to cause him great anxiety, yet
they had a very quick run. They sailed from Miramichi in the
evening and early next morning were at Bedeque. But the most remarkable instance of the preserving care of divine Providence which
he ever experienced, was on a visit to the same place in the year
1817, in company with Dr. McGregor, with whom he was sent to conduct the Rev. James Thomson. They took passage from Pictou in
a new vessel, which was going to Miramichi to take in cargo. The
vessel had not sufficient ballast, but they had a pleasant voyage over,
and dreamed not of danger. But scarcely had they landed from her
till she capsized in the river, filled and sunk to the bottom, and was
afterwards raised only with great difficulty. We regret that we have
it not in our power to give a fuller account of his missionary labors,
but what we have said will be sufficient to show how applicable to
him was the language of the apostle, "In journeyings often, in perils
of waters, in perils of robbers, in perils by mine own countrymen, in
perils by the heathen, in perils in the city, in perils in the wilderness,
in perils on the sea, in perils among false brethren; in weariness and
painfulness, in watching often, in hunger and thirst, in fastings often,
in cold and nakedness. Beside, those things that are without, that
which cometh upon me daily, the care of all the churches."

VIII. CONGREGATIONAL CHANGES.

Under the pastoral labors which we have already described, his
congregation gradually increased, both in numbers and religious
knowledge, so that it soon became necessary to seek additional ministerial labor in it. It has sometimes been the case that ministers
have shown a reluctance to part with any portion of their congregation. Sometimes this has arisen from a fear that being but imperfectly

supplied by the whole, they must be much worse off it dependent on the half. Such a view, however, is found in practice to be quite erroneous. Mininisters after the division of their congregation have found themselves better supported by the half than they were previously by the whole, we suppose somewhat upon the same principle by which a farmer derives more produce from a small piece of ground well tilled, than he would have done from double the same surface imperfectly labored. The plan, too, of a minister scattering his labors over a wide extent of country, is injurious to the interests of the congregation. "The great extent of congregation," says the Rev. R. S. Patterson, "is a serious injury to the interests of religion. The minister having many preaching places, can be present at each only once in the course of a number of Sabbaths. The people being for a length of time without preaching, are apt to become careless, or to be led away by intruders. This, however, is an evil which, in a new country cannot be altogether avoided. The inhabitants being few in each locality, are not able to maintain a minister. It is of importance, however, as soon as the population increases, that the outposts should be detached and formed into seperate congregations. Such was the wise course pursued by Dr. Keir. At first his congregation was scattered over a very wide extent of country. As the population became more dense, and the members of the church increased, various parts were detached and formed into new congregations, until Princetown alone remained under his pastoral care."

The changes will be best described by quoting his own words in reply to the address of the congregation at his Jubilee in 1858. "The first part that was disjoined and erected into a separate congregation was Richmond Bay, comprising Lots No. 13, 14, 16, 17, which took place in the year 1819, when it was placed under the pastoral inspection of the Rev. Andrew Nicol, an ordained minister from the Associate Synod of Scotland. His continuance in the charge, however, was short, for he died in about a year after his induction, and the congregation was left vacant. Bedeque was next disjoined, and erected into a separate congregation, and in connexion with the vacant congregation of Richmond Bay, was put under the pastoral charge of Mr. William McGregor, a preacher who had arrived from the General Associate Synod in Scotland in 1820, and was ordained and inducted on the 11th of October, in the year 1821.

" In about three years after his induction Mr. McGregor demitted his charge of the congregation at Bedeque, which for a short time was again supplied with the ....

minister, with your consent, in the same proportion as it had been before its separation. On the 22nd of March 1829, the Rev. R. S. Patterson, who had previously received a unanimous call, was admitted to the pastoral charge of the congregation of Bedeque From that period the congregation of Princetown continued to consist of Princetown Royalty, and New London, with the adjacent settlements of Cavendish and New Glasgow, because there had been previously a large accession of membership by immigration at two different times, first, from the Highlands of Scotland to New London, and secondly from the Clyde to New Glasgow.

" But in the year 1827, the Presbyterian population in the last mentioned settlements were disjoined from the Princetown congregation, and erected into a new congregation, and put under the pastoral charge of the Rev. Hugh Dunbar. From that period until the present time, being the space of thirty-one years, the congregation of Princetown has enjoyed a regular dispensation of gospel ordinances in one place of worship, the locality being about ten miles square, the number of adherents, of general attendance, and of communicants being greater than before the other congregations were disjoined from it. •

" It may be observed here that the congregation of Cascumpeque, now under the pastoral inspection of the Rev. Allan Fraser, though at no time, properly speaking, in connexion, as forming any part of the Princetown congregation, yet it has in a certain sense sprung from it, as it has received many of its members, and has been supplied from it at an early period with a dispensation of gospel ordinances."

To these it may be added that a portion of the congregation of New London separated from it and united with the Scottish Establishment, and afterward with the Free Church, which would be the sixth Presbyterian congregation formed out of his original charge. And as one of them is nearly ripe for division there will soon be seven.

It is scarcely necessary to remark that during this time the state of the country underwent similar changes. The forest yielded to the axe of the settler, and the wilderness became a fruitful field. The rude hut of the dweller in the wood was exchanged for the comfortable inhabitation, and the difficulties of travelling passed away. The rivers were bridged and the broad carriage road rendered the travelling in his own congregation, and intercourse with other places comparatively easy.

It must be remembered that during the whole course of his minis-

try unbrok a harmony prevailed between him and his congregation
There were no doubt, trials in the case of individuals, but the Great
Head of the Church never suffered to spring up any of those " roots
of bitterness" by which "many are defiled." And not only so but the
people evinced the warmest attachment to him. This feeling was
strong in those sections, which it was deemed advisable to erect into
new congregations. In not a single instance did the separation take
place from anything like bad feeling. On the contrary, the people
in the districts disjoined agreed to it only with great reluctance, and
retained the warmest feelings of attachment to him. Many would
enter into the feelings expressed by Wm. McNeil Esq., of Cavendish,
at the Jubilee: " He had always regretted being disjoined from Dr.
Kier; he was opposed to the measure. Perhaps it was selfish in him
to be so. But it had been considered for the benefit of the church."
And in the more immediate sphere of his labors, he was the object
of an amount of veneration and attachment, which might have filled
with self-elation any person, but one In whom the grace of God
reigned in the production of such unfeigned humility. We cannot
however commend their financial arrangements, regarding him. In
the first year of his ministry their conduct would compare favorably
with the other congregations of the church. Indeed his congregation
not long after his settlement took the lead in raising their minister's
salary. But of late years, while the expense of living has increased,
they have allowed themselves to be outstripped by younger congre-
gregations, and have retained modes of dealing with the minister,
which though well enough fifty years ago, are now far behind the
age. We have been grieved to see such an old and worthy servant
of Christ with a considerable family receiving from a congregation
among whom he had spent the prime of his strength, less than a
number of mere striplings trained under him, were receiving from
weaker congregations, even while they had no person dependent on
them. Nor was it creditable that while the latter were receiving
their salary in cash, and at regular times, he had to submit to a system of irregular produce payment, condemned by the synod, and ex-
ploded in almost every congregation of the body. We do not say
that this was altogether attributable to them. It was partly owing
to his own disinterested disregard of worldly things. He had "learned in whatever state he was therewith to be content," and he troubled them not with any appeals regarding his own salary. Certain-
ly however their conduct arose from no want of attachment to him,
but from an imperfect knowledge of their duty

We must also remark, that during the whole course of his ministry, the efforts of Sectarians to introduce division into his congregation and build up their own party principles upon the ruins of its peace, were entirely unsuccessful. Most of our Presbyterian congregations have been assailed in this manner. There are always parties professing that their object is to preach the gospel of Christ, but who instead of doing this where he is not known, confine their labors to those already blessed with the ministrations of faithful servants of Christ; and instead of directing their efforts to the conversion of sinners to the Saviour, devote their energies to bringing men from the Presbyterian fold into their own, sometimes on the ground that Presbyterians when gained over, make the very best members they have, which amounts to a confession, that our system is the means of making more efficient Christians than theirs. These men are not always very scrupulous as to the means they employ. The dissatisfaction of an individual, whose conduct may have brought him under the discipline of the Church, or of some self-conceited person, who imagines that he has not received the attention he deserves, will form a point, on which they alight like carrion fowls on corruption, and by flattery, or making themselves " all things to all men," in another sense than the apostle Paul, they will commonly succeed in gaining some, and strife and division ensue. All this will be done under the pretence of love and peace. All the other Presbyterian congregations in the Island had suffered more or less from these "spiritual kidnappers," as John Angel James called them, but against Dr. Keir, their efforts fell harmless as the arrow from the solid rock. All their plans were ineffectual to excite division among his people. Some of them felt considerably chagrined, that they were thus so entirely baffled; and within the last two or three years, when there were indications of failing strength on the part of Dr. Keir, their hopes of success revived, and they began again "creeping in," with the hope of securing their purpose. We are happy to say, that in spite of such kind attentions to their spiritual interests, the congregation has remained united and harmonious. Long may they continue so. To them we say, " Be of one mind, live in peace, and the God of peace shall be with you." And with this view guard against those Sectarian Proselytizers, who would compass sea and land to make one proselite, "and when they have made him, he is two fold more the child of Hell than he was before." "Mark them which cause divisions and offences among you contrary to the doctrine ye have learned; and avoid them. For they that are such, serve not our Lord Jesus Christ, but their own belly; and by good words and fair speeches deceive the hearts of the people."

IX. Presbytery of P. E. Island Formed and his Conduct as a Minister thereof.

One of the greatest losses which he suffered and perhaps we might say one of the severest trials he endured, during the early years of his ministerial life, was the want of brethren near him with whom he could take sweet counsel, and whose co-operation and sympathy might strengthen his hands. "Iron sharpeneth iron, so a man's countenance his friend," but he like Abraham, had gone forth alone. For some years there was not a ministerial brother on the Island, and when one did come, it was not long till he was separated from his congregation, and Dr. Keir left alone. During this time he was connected with the Presbytery of Pictou, but such was the difficulty of intercourse, that he rarely met with it in Presbytery. There was no steamer wafting the traveller swiftly, and with regularity to his destination. Not only weeks but months elapsed without any communication with the main land. He informed us that on one occasion, when war broke out, several months elapsed before the people on the Island heard of it. The Presbytery, however, did what they could to hold intercourse with him and to strengthen his hands by brotherly countenance. Almost every summer one or other of the brethren of that Presbytery went over on a missionary excursion.— In this Dr. McGregor was especially forward. On such occasions the Lord's Supper was dispensed, and he enjoyed a season of hallowed fraternal intercourse. When the Synod was formed in 1817, he generally had the privilege of meeting his brethren once a year, as by this time sailing packets had been established between P. E. Island and Nova Scotia. But still he was in a great measure cut off from the church. At length he was to see a Presbytery formed, where he had been a solitary laborer. We shall again quote the words of Mr. Patterson.

"Previous to the settlement of Mr. McGregor at Richmond Bay, there had been no Presbytery in the Island. But on October 11th, 1821, the day of Mr. McGregor's ordination, in accordance with a deed of Synod, the Presbytery of P. E. Island was constituted, and held its first meeting at Richmond Bay.* The members present were Rev. Dr. Keir, of Princetown, who was chosen first moderator, the Rev. Robert Douglass, of St. Peters,† the Rev. William McGregor of Richmond Bay, ministers; and Edward Ramsay, Ruling Elder. The formation of a Presbytery was an event of deep interest to the friends

* At Lot 16.
† Mr. Douglass had been inducted a few days previously.

of the church in general. In particular in the mind of Dr. Keir, it excited the most heartfelt satisfaction and the most fervent gratitude to God. Far removed from any brother with whom he could consult in the moment of perplexity, he had been almost a solitary laborer.— Two brother ministers* he had seen, in the mysterious Providence of God, snatched away by the relentless hand of death. Another, through dissatisfaction arising between him and his congregation, had been loosed from the pastoral relation. But now he had the satisfaction to be associated with brethren, whom he could consult in difficulties, who would be fellow-laborers in the wide field which he had occupied, and would water where he had planted. No sooner was a Presbytery formed, than applications for supply of preaching were presented from Murray Harbour, in King's County, and Shimogue in New Brunswick."

The Presbytery directed its attention earnestly to the work of supplying the destitute portions of the Island with the word of life, and soon increased in number. But the extension of the church was much hindered, as it has been almost ever since, by the want of ministers. We wish however to notice particularly, that in all its efforts Dr. Keir took a most active part. Whatever labors devolved upon its members, ho cheerfully bore his full share. In attendance upon its meetings he was regular and conscientious. Only the most serious obstacles could prevent his being present. This was the case with him to the very last year of his life. Indeed his brethren were often astonished at his presence, when the distance from the place of meeting, the inclemency of the weather or the badness of the roads might have furnished a sufficient excuse for his absence. Indeed his conduct in this respect was often a reproof to younger men, who allow trifling difficulties to prevent their attendance on these meetings, so important to the church and so useful to themselves.

From the formation of the Presbytery he was regarded by the members as a father among them. He was not only the oldest minister, but his position had given him a large amount of experience, his apostolic character excited their affection and esteem, and his practical good sense rendered his counsel valuable. Hence from the very first formation of the Presbytery all its members looked to him with peculiar veneration. He lived to see these brethren and others who joined it afterward committed to the silent tomb; but their places were filled by younger men, to all of whom he was a father and a friend, not indeed assuming any

---

* The Rev'ds. Peter Gordon and Andrew Nicol.

airs of authority from his years and position, but ever ready to yield his counsel, sympathy or assistance. Very properly then did the members of Presbytery, on the occasion of his jubilee, address him in the following terms: "Especially do we feel it our duty as co-presbyters to express our esteem of your conduct as a member of Presbytery. As such you have been distinguished by uniform kindness and brotherly feeling— by readiness to co-operate in every good work; and we have all reason to acknowledge our personal obligations for the fatherly interest you have taken in us and for the counsel and assistance, which you have always been ready to impart, and the value of which we have had reason to feel."

X. His Professorial Labors.

We have now to exhibit Dr. Keir in a different position—one in some respects of higher usefulness, at all events of greater importance to the church at large. Dr. McCulloch having been removed from the church on earth in the year 1843, Dr. Keir was at the meeting of the Synod in the summer following chosen his successor. For the discharge of the duties of this office, it must be acknowledged that Dr. Keir was under considerable disadvantages. He had been in a situation, where he had but little access to books, except his own library, and his limited salary had not enabled him to gather a large collection. Indeed with the productions of recent writers, orthodox or heretical, he had scarcely had any opportunity of being familiar. Besides, his life had been devoted to pastoral labors of a kind, which required so much time and involved such an amount of physical toil, that in the matter of study, he could do little more than attend to what was absolutely necessary for his congregational work. Under these circumstances, his acquaintance with that higher range of study, with which it is expected that a professor should be versant, was necessarily limited. From the date of his settlement, even the study of the sacred languages, had not been prosecuted with any degree of constancy or regularity; and he was at an age when men generally do not enter upon a new course of study. These disadvantages he felt strongly himself, and it was therefore with some difficulty that he could be persuaded to undertake the office.

But on the other hand, if he had not attended to the forms in which Theology had been presented by modern writers, he was abundantly familiar with its matter, as exhibited on the writings of the great standard divines of the 17th century in England, and of the Marrowmen and the Secession fathers in Scotland on the 18th. We conceive the writings of the former to form a complete storehouse of Theology, and the man who has his quiver filled with weapons drawn from that armory, is well equipped for warfare against the armies of the aliens. Desirable as it is to be acquainted with modern Theological writers, yet the old seem to have pushed their enquiries to the full limits of the powers of the human mind, and often times the productions of modern orthodox writers, are but a sort of *detritus* of their writings, while the ingenuity of modern errorists has scarcely forged any new weapons of assault upon divine truth. The Marrowmen and Secession fathers, who have been called "the only distinctive school of Theology that Scotland has produced," exhibit in substance the same system, though slightly modified in the mode of its presentation. With the views of these writers, Dr. Keir's acquaintance was both accurate and extensive. We may here remark, that so far as his Theology was formed from any human writings, it might be said to have been moulded by the authors referred to. His Theology was that of Owen and the Secession fathers. While we say this, we must however remark, that after all his Theology was essential Biblical. His views were drawn directly from the great fountain of divine truth, and all his expositions of doctrines were distinguished by their fulness of scripture reference. He was indeed a man "mighty in the scriptures." In his preaching too he had treated the great doctrines of the gospel systematically, and had a course of sermons, which presented nearly a complete system of Theology. Thus he was equipped for the duties of the office in a manner, which amply justified the synod's choice.

Having with some reluctance accepted the office, he entered upon its duties with great diligence. He devoted his attention to such reading, as would enable him to keep abreast of the Christian Literature of the age; and he extended the sermons referred to into a full course of lectures on Theology, of which a synopsis has been published for the use of his students. In many Institutions at the present day, from the number of excellent systems of Theology already before the public, it is not considered the most efficient mode of teaching Theology, for the Professor to prepare a full course of lectures of his own. It is believed that the work may be done as thoroughly by examination of the students on one of the standard systems, such as Dick's, and by supplementary lectures on particular subjects, that may require special consideration. Dr. Keir had been accustomed to the other mode, and his course of lectures will afford the best evidence of his assiduity It was not our privilege to hear his lectures as written out, nor can we speak of their contents from personal knowledge of them otherwise. But from what we have heard we believe that they afford most creditable evidence not only of the soundness of his views, but also of the extent of his Theological attainments.

For a few years after his appointment, the Hall met in his house, and the students, who were then few in number, boarded with his family. It is only of this period, that we can speak from our own experience, and we believe that we express the feeling of those, not a numerous body, who attended at that time, when we say that we reckon the few weeks spent annually with him in this way as not only among the most pleasant, but also as among the most valuable, for our Christian progress and ministerial usefulness, of our past lives. We attended daily upon his prelections, and he gave us plenty of work to do, so that we were kept busy. As a lecturer we do not profess to set him along side of some we have heard in other Institutions. We have sat under men of greater originality of thought, men who impressed us more deeply with a sense of their intellectual power—we have heard lectures from such men, showing a wider range of thought, taking a firmer grasp of a subject and exhibiting it in more brilliant lights; but we have never sat under one, who produced deeper impressions of moral goodness, nor one who in the handling of the great themes of Christian doctrine, presented them more as great practical realities—nor one who left deeper impressions on our minds of the duties and responsibilities of the sacred office.— Indeed we confess that we consider Dr. Keir's excellence as a professor lay rather in this point, than either in the learning or intellectual power displayed on his prelections.

Impressions of this kind were greatly deepened by the privilege we then enjoyed, not only of daily, but we may say of hourly personal intercourse with him. It was then that we learned rightly to estimate his worth, and associating with him thus closely, we must have been slow scholars, if we did not come away better men and better fitted for usefulness as ministers. Then too it may·be observed we learned the extent both of his Theological attainments and general information. From hesitancy of manner and his great natural modesty, his public appearances often did not do justice to himself, and did not leave the most favourable impressions upon the mind of strangers. Those only who were brought into familiar intercourse with him in private, fully knew the loveliness of his character, and the extent of his acquirements.

In subsequent years the Hall met at West River, and we cannot speak of his teaching there from personal experience. But his faith fulness and success as a Theological tutor, will best appear in those who, trained under him, are now preaching the gospel of God's Son, not only in this Province, but in the distant isles of the sea. Notwithstanding the disadvantages un which they have been placed, he might say as Dr. Balmer, "Happy is the man that hath his quiver full of them."

X. CHRISTIAN AND BENEVOLENT ENTERPRISE.

In noticing Dr. Keir's public labors, there remains only one other point to be considered, viz: the interest which he took in the Christian and benevolent enterprises of the age. To this however we can but briefly advert. From an early period he had been deeply interested in the Missionary undertakings of the church, and in the true spirit of Missionary devotedness, he had given himself to the work of preaching the gospel in America. And he ever after manifested how deeply his heart was engaged in every thing connected with the prosperity of Zion and the extension of the kingdom of the Redeemer.

During the first years of his ministry, so far as we aware, it does not appear that to any considerable extent, he led his congregation to contribute either to the schemes of the church, or to the great religious institutions of the age. His congregation was weak, its members scattered and scarcely able to support the ordinances of religion among themselves; and money was especially scarce, Prince Edward Island, more than any other part of the church, having, even when blessed with abundance of food, hitherto always had difficulty in securing a *moneyed* circulating medium, wheat, oats, barley, having often been the regular articles of exchange.

But he always felt an interest in the work of gospel diffusion, and in later years he entered with his whole heart, into the work of exciting his own congregation and others to liberality in the great work. He particularly delighted in the Foreign Mission of our church. After Mr. Geddie he was one of the first in the body to adopt the idea, and to believe in its practicability. By the influence of his exhortations and the example of his liberality, his congregation were led to come under most liberal engagements, in the event of the synod's entering upon such an undertaking. He introduced the overture for engaging in the work into synod and the weight of his character and opinion contributed much to the carrying of the measure. It was a day of deep delight to him when the church finally engaged in the work. We were present at the Presbytery, when Mr

Geddie was finally separated from his congregation, and at a public meeting held the same day in the Princetown church to bid him farewell. Amid many things that were interesting and affecting, we can yet well recollect the appearance of Dr. Keir on the occasion. To him the whole scene, especially when viewed in connexion with the past, excited strong emotions. In a few, but deeply impressive words, he contrasted what they now saw with the state of things when he arrived on the Island. Thirty-seven years before he had left his native land as a Foreign Missionary, and thirty-five years before he had been ordained over a people few in number, widely scattered, and pinched in their worldly circumstances, and for a time was the only Presbyterian minister on Prince Edward Island. Now he saw a number of flourishing congregations, and many faithful ministers of different denominations throughout the Island, and now the church to which he belonged, principally through the zeal of the ministers, and the liberality of the congregations, in that section of it, engaged in sending a minister to labor far hence among the Gentiles,—an undertaking at that time almost unprecedented among colonial churches. With strong feeling of gratitude might he say, 'what hath God wrought?'

In the carrying on of the work, he was ever ready to render his counsel and assistance. He was a member of the Foreign Mission Board from its formation till his death, and so far as he was enabled to attend its meetings, took an active part in the management of its business. The progress of the mission he anxiously watched, and even in its darkest hour, his faith in the promises of the God of Missions, and his confidence in its success were never shaken. Firmly did he anticipate the day, when the spirit of God would descend upon the moral desert, and the thirsty land become pools of water. When the clouds began to break, and when tidings of success refreshed our hearts, and still more when each succeeding message brought us intelligence of additional progress, none rejoiced more than Dr. Keir, or more heartily raised his voice in giving glory to him who alone giveth the increase.

XII. Personal and Domestic History.

Having thus briefly sketched his chief public efforts, we must briefly refer to his personal and domestic history. Upon this there is not much to record. Of his religious history we can say but little. He kept no diary and he did not proclaim his piety on the housetops, by an ostentatious declaration of his "experience." But his close walk with God and his growing likeness to the Saviour were clearly manifest. Those who knew him intimately knew how close was daily communion with his heavenly father. But to all who came in contact with him, it was evident that his path like that of the just, was shining more and more unto the perfect day. We have heard it said that in youth his temper was quick. If so grace enabled him to subdue it so entirely, that he was distinguished for his Christian meekness—but all the features of the Christian character were exhibited in increasing brilliancy, so as to be known and read of all men.

He was never a very strong man, and some thirty years ago he exhibited signs of failing strength, which alarmed his friends. But from this he recovered and through the greater part of his ministerial career, he enjoyed an amount of health, which enabled him to discharge the duties of the ministry with an uninterrupted regularity, such as has been rarely exhibited. " It is worthy of being remembered, here also," he remarked at his Jubilee "as no ordinary ground of thankfulness that during the whole of this long period, (of fifty years) I have not been prevented by sickness, but only upon two occasions, from preaching every Lord's day, and at all other times, when called in Providence to the performance of the duty." We may mention that one of these occasions was after he had passed his 77th year.

We do not feel it necessary to draw aside the veil from his private life, and to expose to public view his appearance in his family. It is sufficient to say that in this relation he exhibited a pattern of the same Christian virtues, as distinguished him in every other walk of life. It has been the case that some excellent men have failed here. But Dr Keir's Christian excellence appeared not so much in the towering eminence of any one feature of character, as in the harmony and proportion in which all the Christian virtues were exhibited. He exhibited not the qualities which make a man extraordinary in one position, but that well balanced state of mind and spirit, which renders a man the object of esteem in all the relations of life. And we say from frequent and favourable opportunities of judging, that those who would see Dr. Keir in his most endearing aspects—those who would have learned how loveable a man he was, and would fully appreciate his excellence, required to see him in the bosom of his family.—It behoved them to observe him as the faithful prophet, priest, and king of that circle—to behold him as the tender husband and the faithful counsellor—as the affectionate father and guide of the young—to mark his firmness in resisting and reproving wrong,

while by love and gentleness he led in the right way, and especially
to behold him as the High priest of the family, presenting their morn
ing and evening sacrifices before the God of the families of the earth
—and they would need to know the place which he occupied in the
hearts of that band.   May they now experience, that "a father of the
fatherless, and the Judge of the widow is God in his holy habitation."
There is scarcely any circumstance in his domestic history requiring
notice in this sketch.   A large family was born to him, among whom
he enjoyed a large measure of "domestic happiness, that only bliss
of paradise, that hath survived the fall;" and he was also called to
endure his share of those trials, which in this life so often rend the
parental heart.   Clouds sometimes darkened his hearth.   But his
trials were borne with resignation, and were made to work together
or good, and under the abundant manifestations of divine goodness
toward him, there was heard in his dwelling "the voice of rejoicing
and of salvation, as there is in the tabernacles of the righteous."

Perhaps we should say here a few words about his preaching.—
From what we have said, it may be at once inferred that the matter
of his discourses would consist of the pure beaten gold of the sanctu
ary.   As a general characteristic, it may be said of them that they
were doctrinal; but they were far from being exclusively so.   His
preaching exhibited a judicious mixture of the doctrinal, the experi-
mental and the practical.   The basis might be doctrinal, but doctrines
were not presented in a dry dogmatic form.   They were always presented as great living truths, lying at the foundation of practical
godliness, and in connexion with his exhibition of them, we have
heard from him some of the most rousing appeals to the conscience,
to which it was ever our privilege to listen.   Like the apostle Paul,
he might be described, as "by *manifestation of the truth commending
himself to every man's conscience in the sight of God.*"   The best testimony to this may be found in the statement of an individual, who
gave up attendance upon his ministrations, assigning as a reason that
he did not like to attend Dr. Keir's preaching, for it always made
him uneasy.   One feature of his discourses is deserving of particular
notice, viz: their biblical character.   Every truth was enforced by
scripture reference, to an extent which showed how deeply he had
drunk at the fountain of wisdom, and how profound his reverence
for divine authority.   It must be admitted however, that his preaching was scarcely of the kind called popular.   This arose partly from
his manner, and in particular from a hesitancy of speech, which was
frequently interrupted by a slight cough, so that strangers, or those
who had only heard him on a few occasions, were often not much

(35)

attracted by it. But any unfavourable impressions produced by his
manner soon passed away, and the judicious and the pious soon
relished the fulness of gospel truth, which he set forth before them in
"good and acceptable words." By some it has been said, that in his
preaching, the "strong meat" predominated to an extent, which rendered it unsuitable for the bulk of ordinary hearers. But the best
proof of the general adaptation of his preaching is to be found in his
congregation, which continued not only their atttachment to himself
personally, but which always felt the warmest admiration for him as
a preacher, and continued to listen with increasing eagerness and
delight, to his ministrations till the very last.

XIII. Old age and Jubilee.

Thus years increased upon him. He had for some time passed the
three score and ten, which form the allotted period of human life, still
he was able to go out and in, discharging the various duties of his sta-
tion. But his old age was what the scriptures emphatically call "a
good old age." It was an old age in a great measure free from bodily
infirmity, in which the senses were left in perfection, and the mind
was still strong, vigorous and cheerful. In his worldly circumstances he was free from the harassing cares of his early years. He
dwelt among his people, and enjoyed largely their esteem and affection, while in every part of the Island, and in other portions of the
church where he was known, his name was mentioned only with the
most loving veneration, while among his brethren in the ministry
he was both loved and venerated as a father. But especially was it
pleasing for him to contemplate the state of the church on the Island
then, compared with what it was when he came to it. "At that period,"
said the Rev. R. S. Patterson writing a few years ago, "the country
presented the appearance of an almost unbroken forest. Only here and
there, at wide intervals, might be seen a few solitary settlers, dwelling
for the most part in poor log huts with a little clearing around them.
The moral and religious condition of the people also was very affecting. The few that made any pretensions to piety, were as sheep
scattered abroad, having no shepherd. The labors of the Rev. Mr.
Gordon had been short, and much impeded by his increasing debility,
even while they did continue. There was therefore little else than
a moral waste when Dr. Keir arrived. But how great the change
which he has lived to witness! Instead of a dense uninterrupted forest,
he sees an extensively cultivated country; instead of a few lonely
huts, numerous and comfortable habitations, instead of a handful of

straggling settlers, a population of over 60,000; instead of a feeble band of isolated Christians, having none to care for their souls, a number of laborious ministers and flourishing congregations. "Ye shall go out with joy, and be led forth with peace; the mountains and the hills shall break forth before you into singing, and all the trees of the forest shall clap their hands. Instead of the thorn, shall come up the fir tree, and instead of the briar shall come up the myrtle tree; and it shall be to the Lord for a name, for an everlasting sign that shall not be cut off."

One trial was indeed permitted to darken his latter days. It was one of a peculiar nature—one in which after all his efforts to clear up the matter, an unfavourable impression regarding his conduct remained upon the minds of many, even of those who were his well-wishers. An extraordinary delusion seized the minds of a multitude of well-meaning people, which could not be dislodged either by fact or argument. This continued for some time, and severely tried his feelings. But Christian faith and patience shone conspicuously under it, and at length God in his Providence gave him ample means of vindicating himself. And though there were still circumstances of grief, yet he had cause for thankfulness, that God "brought forth his righteousness as the light and his loving-kindness as the noon-day."

Of Dr. Keir it may be said emphatically that his last days were his best days. His character exhibited a beautiful picture of ripeness for the master's garner, and meetness for the inheritance of the saints in light; while he continued to discharge all the labors of the ministry, and in a manner, which if not in bodily vigor, yet in mental and moral power, surpassed the performances of his early days.— Even last winter he went through the whole work, of family visitation in his congregation. In him was fulfilled the promise; the "righteous shall flourish like the Palm tree; he shall grow like a cedar in Lebanon. Those that be planted in the house of the Lord shall flourish in the courts of our God. They shall still bring fruit in old age; they shall be fat and flourishing; to shew that the Lord is upright, he is my rock, and there is no unrighteousness in him."

In July last the congregation of Princetown resolved to celebrate his Jubilee. It is usual to date a person's ministry from his ordination. But as Dr. Keir had commenced to labor in Princetown in 1808, and had continued with but slight interruptions to minister there ever since, although his ordination did not take place for some time after, it was resolved to celebrate his Jubilee then. As events have been ordered since, we cannot but rejoice at their determination.—

The event excited great interest through the Island. On the day appointed, (20th July,) the whole country round poured forth a stream of carriages and horsemen, in some places all the carriages and horses in the settlement being put in requisition. A number living at a distance had arrived in Princetown the day previous, and from an early hour in the day, crowds were to be seen gathering from every direction. Tea had been set out in the upper and lower stories of the Mechanic's Institute, and in an arbor adjoining, as well as in another building near. Tables had been spread for 450 guests, and these were filled four times, and part of them five times. It was believed that many were present who did not partake of the good things, provided in such abundance by the people of Princetown. It was calculated that there must have been 3000 persons present.— They were from all parts of the Island, some having come all the way from Cascumpeque on the west, and from Belfast on the east.— They were of all denominations of professing christians. Even a number of Roman Catholics were present.

After tea the company met in the open air. After religious exercises addresses were presented to Dr. Keir from the congregation of Princetown and the Presbytery of P. E. Island, to which he made suitable replies. The audience was then addressed by several ministers present, when several votes of thanks were passed, the doxology was sung, and the congregation was dismissed with the Apostolic benediction, when the vast crowds quietly separated, all seemingly gratified with what they had witnessed. The proceeds of the Tea meeting amounting to £112, were handed over to Dr. Keir as an expression of good will.

XIV. LAST DAYS, DEATH AND BURIAL.

At the time of his Jubilee, Dr. Keir appeared in his usual health. A pensive thoughtfulness, deeper than usual, appeared to rest upon him, but it seemed only appropriate to the tender recollections of the past, and those views of the solemn responsibilities of his ministry, which the occasion would naturally suggest. But there was nothing to indicate, that his health was worse than it had been for years, or that it might not be his Master's will to continue him in active service for some years to come. He continued to discharge the duties of his pastorate till the time for the opening of the Seminary. But it was remarked that for some time before his death, his pulpit ministrations were marked by more than usual earnestness. He seemed to feel, more and more deeply the value of the soul, the shortness

and uncertainty of life, and the nearness of eternity, and he preached
as if already he were breathing the air of the better land, to which
he was so soon to take his journey. On the Sabbath before leaving
home, the last of his earthly ministry, he lectured on that exclama-
tion in which the apostle, concluding his exposition of the grander
themes of Salvation—pours forth his sublime and affecting tri-
bute to the wisdom, goodness and sovereignty of God—in a strain
scarcely surpassed even in Scripture—a passage, which might well
have been chosen as a fitting close to the ministry of one, who had
been called to teach divine truth as a system, and whose great aim in
all his instructions had been to exhibit God as all in all, Rom. xi. 33
—36, " O the depth of the riches both of the wisdom and knowledge
of God! how unsearchable are his judgments, and his ways past
finding out! For who hath known the mind of the Lord? or who
hath been his counsellor? or who hath first given to him, and it shall
be recompensed unto him again? For of him and through him, and
to him, are all things; to whom be glory for ever, Amen."

At the end of August he came over to the mainland, to enter upon
the duties of the Theological Hall. He attended the opening of the
Seminary in the new buildings at Truro on the 1st of September,
and entered upon the duties of his class, seemingly in his usual state
of health. The only circumstance remarked in the conducting of his
class, which would give indication of anything the matter with him,
was that at times his mind seemed in a state of vacancy, until arous
ed by something said or done in his presence. But the same thing
had been noted before, though perhaps not to the same extent,
and it did not excite attention. He went through the exercises of
the class as usual until the 15th of the month. On that day after
class he went to the Post office to enquire for letters from home, but
while away lost all recollection. He fell into the hands of kind
friends, who conveyed him to his lodgings in a carriage. Medical
aid was called on, and every thing was done for him that human
skill could devise. But congestion of the brain had set in, and his
constitution was too far gone to resist its violence. In spite of all
that medical skill could do, he continued to sink till about 12 o'clock
on the night of the 22nd, when he expired. His work was done.—
His Great Master had given the commission and none could reverse
his decision.

During the greater part of his illness he was in a state of lethargy,
which continued to deepen till the end, so that he held but little
communication with any person. When spoken to in a loud or
sharp tone of voice, he was aroused for an instant, and was able to

give an intelligent answer, but immediately he relapsed again into unconsciousness, and the impression made at the moment seemed as rapidly to be effaced. Thus there was no opportunity of his giving one of those death-bed testimonies, which good men are often permitted to bear to the honor of our religion. He was not permitted to utter any of those triumphant expressions of joy and hope, so comforting to friends, and by which

> The chamber were the good man meets his fate
> Is privileged beyond the common walk of life,
> Quite on the verge of heaven.

Nor was he permitted to utter any of those parting counsels and warnings so well fitted to be profitable to survivors. But there was no need of such in his case. His life of abundant labors is a better testimony than any death-bed saying. " Blessed are the dead that die in the Lord from henceforth, yea, saith the spirit, they rest from their labors, and *their works do follow them*."

It would no doubt have been a pleasure to his friends had he been permitted to die in the bosom of his own family. But seeing that his master willed otherwise, they are called to bow in submission to his will, and say "It is the Lord, let him do what seemeth him good." Perhaps they may even here see reason to say of this as of all his arrangements, "he hath done all things well." We think it was appropriate to a long and laborious life, that he should die *at his post* with all his armor on, and still "about his father's business."

Intelligence of his sickness had been conveyed to his family, but not in time for any of them, with the exception of his youngest son, who happened to be in Nova Scotia, to reach Truro before he died. Some members of the family came from Princetown to Charlottetown, intending to come across, but the steamer had gone and no other mode of conveyance offered. They however heard of him frequently by telegraph, and during the two or three days that elapsed till intelligence of his death was received, the house at which they lodged was a house of mourning, many who had sat under his ministry, and many belonging to the city, who had known him and venerated his character, calling frequently and anxiously enquiring for tidings regarding him, and giving utterance to sincere expressions of sorrow, when they heard that all was over. When they returned home, the house was filled with persons who had assembled to condole with the family, and when the tidings were conveyed, that the husband, the father, and the pastor, was now no more, the scene was deeply affecting. But this we must pass over.

In the meantime arrangements had been made for the removal of the remains to Princetown for interment. On the day following his death, (Thursday 23rd September,) they were conveyed to Pictou, being followed that distance by the students at the Hall. There they were placed on board the steamer Westmorland. What followed we shall give in the words of Rev. R. S. Patterson: .

"On Thursday, the 23rd of September, I first learned of the alarming illness of Dr. Keir. On Friday one of the Elders of the Princetown congregation, called at my house and informed me of his death, and that he was on his way to Summerside, where his remains were expected by the steamer *Westmorland* that day. I accompanied the Elder to Summerside, on approaching which place I perceived a larger than usual number of persons collected there. On coming near, I recognized many members of the congregation of Princetown, who had come to meet the remains of their deceased pastor, and accompany them to his late residence. Deep sorrow was depicted upon every countenance, and among the first words which I heard from many lips were these: "O, we have sustained a great loss! There were many persons, however, from other places, as well as from Princetown. All seemed to vie with one another in testifying their respect for the deceased.

"At about four o'clock the steamer was seen in the distance and rapidly neared the wharf, her colors being half-mast high. A greater crowd of persons were assembled at the landing, then had ever been seen upon any previous arrival of the boat. The remains being landed and placed in a suitable vehicle, the procession moved slowly toward Princetown. Sixty-two carriages, containing persons belonging to his congregation, followed the remains of Dr. Keir from Summerside to his late residence, which was very remarkable, considering that the intelligence of his decease had reached Princetown, only on the previous night. As the procession moved towards Princetown, groups of persons were to be seen along the road in various places, indicating the intense interest everywhere felt in regard to the deceased. It was sometime after dark before we arrived at the late residence of Dr. Keir. Previous to the introduction of the remains into the house, I entered for the purpose of endeavouring to administer suitable consolation to the bereaved family. I found a large company of persons, chiefly females, present who had come to await the arrival of the procession. It was evident from their countenances that they felt that they had sustained a severe bereavement. The remains were brought into the house, and on the following morning, Saturday, the coffin was uncovered, and the bereaved family had the melancholy satisfaction of looking upon the countenance, now pale in death, of the once affectionate husband and revered and kind father, and the congregation, of their lamented pastor. No provision had been made for sermon on the following Sabbath. The funeral was appointed to take place on Monday ensuing at two o'clock.

"On Monday I proceeded to Princetown, whence I had returned home on Saturday. A large number of persons had assembled to the funeral, how many we have no means of exactly knowing. Besides many from the neighboring settlements, scarcely any in the congregation was absent, that could possibly be present. Not a few Roman Catholics, also, attended the funeral. The services were commenced by singing a part of the 39th Psalm, which was given out by the Rev. Isaac Murray, who also read the 15th Chapter of 1st Corinthians. I then offered up prayer. The people having taken some refreshment, prayer was again offered up, in a very impressive manner, by the Rev. Alex. Sutherland, of the Free Church, who had kindly come from a considerable distance to be present upon the occasion. The remains were then conveyed to the resting place in the church-yard, and there deposited. As I had been appointed by the Presbytery to supply the pulpit at Princetown, on the following Sabbath, I endeavored to improve the solemn event by a sermon from Matthew xxiv; 45, 46. "Who then is a faithful and wise and servant, whom the Lord hath appointed ruler over his house to give them meat in due season ; blessed is that servant, whom his Lord when he cometh shall find so doing."

(41

XV. Conclusion.

We have thus sketched the history of a good man lately passed from our midst—we have given an outline of his labors, and perhaps now we should endeavor to delineate his character; but this will be better exhibited by the above memorial of his life, imperfect as it is, than by any thing we can say here. Nor do we feel it necessary, to say much in the way of describing his intellectual powers. We by no means place Dr Keir in the first rank as to talents or original genius. And yet he occupied a place in our Church, such as no other man has done for some time. We are safe in saying that for a number of years there has been no member of our Synod who had the general esteem and veneration of his brethren, to the extent which he had, or whose words carried greater influence. To what was this attributable? In part no doubt it was owing to his years and long and faithful services in the Church: but there must have been something in the man himself to win such a position. We can barely enumerate what we regard as the leading qualities of his mind, by the combination of which he became so honorable among his brethren. In the first place, he possessed, not extraordinary powers of mind, yet good talents, among which predominated that mysterious faculty, or whatever it may be called, in which men of great talents are sometimes deficient, generally known as good common sense. To this may be traced that practical prudence, which through life distinguished him, and which rendered him so useful as a practical man in the Church. But secondly, he was characterized by great diligence, all his powers were well improved, and whatever his hand formed to do he did it with his might. And thirdly, his whole conduct bore the impress of deep piety. In his presence, we felt "how awful goodness is." His religion especially manifested itself in the kindness and affection of his disposition. His whole intercourse with men seemed to be guided by the command of the Apostle, "Giving none offence, either to Jew or Gentile, that the ministry be not blamed." And lastly, he was distinguished by great devotedness to his work. This in one view, may be regarded as a part of piety, but in another it is one peculiar form in which it manifests itself. It is now universally acknowledged, that no man will excel in any profession, or department of business, without a spirit of devotedness to it, and this spirit will supply in a good measure, the lack of other qualifications. The predominant quality of Dr Keir's mind was "*devotedness to the service of God in the gospel of his Son,*" and we believe that to this, especially combined with the features already mentioned, was owing the fact, that he became " more honorable than his brethren."

The subject suggests many practical reflections. We shall however. in conclusion give only some thoughts on the death of an aged minister, extracted from a sermon by the Rev. J. Kerr of Glasgow, on the death of his colleague, Dr Kidston.

"The world we live in, is one of ceaseless mutation. Every setting sun brings its changes whether we perceive them or not. Day by day, "our age is departed and removed from us like a shepherd's tent." We pitch our tabernacle every night nearer death, nearer judgement. The departure of each friend who enters the world of spirits is intended to give us this admonition. Leaving, they leave this lesson, "Thou also shalt become weak as we ; thou shalt become like unto us." The death of a Christian minister comes with a wide circumference and deeper significance of warning than almost any other. It visits every house in a large community with its note of change, and knocks loudly at every heart. The pulpit speaks in death, as in life, to all who gather round it. The absence of its wonted occupant is the last and most solemn of his admonitions—the silent eloquence of that preacher, Death—who more impressively than the wise man, writes "vanity of vanities," on all this sublunary life. The departure of an aged minister gives an emphasis to this lesson even more profound. For sixty years, change invaded every seat in the house of God, but it spared the central one. The teachers placed seemed to have made covenant with death, a stranger might have visited this congregation at the interval of half a century to find the same face there, and in the useless revolutions around it, one fixed place appeared to have been found, as the firmament of stars, moveless amid surrounding mutability. But now that they is dissolved, the ancient landmark is removed which these fathers had set for us. Now we have been brought to the heartfelt acknowledgement, "We are strangers before thee and sojourners, as were all our fathers : our days on the earth are as a shadow, and there is none abiding." This one change calls to mind many ; it stirs up the dead for us ; it leads the eyes to wander from seat to seat, and ask the question, "Our fathers, where are they." There are high places of weeping in the path of life that summon us to look back, and none more sacred and touching, than those that lead us to meditate on the waste that death has caused in a religious community. The overthrow of empires and fall of ancient dynasties are impressive ; and yet frequently they roll over head like the thunder peal, and leave the homes of men unharmed, that the sun may smile on them when the storm is past. But a change in a Christian congregation reminds us of the quenching of domestic fires, of the dispersions of family circles, of coldness and desolation in homes and hearts." * * *

"While we cast our eyes further back, how few survive of those that saw him who has just departed enter on his ministry ! The names of them that are asleep are more by far than of them who are alive and remain. 'Tis long since the congregation of the dead has had the majority. Men of faith and prayer and active zeal, who carried many a year the ark of God, are numbered with a generation past. Families once numerous, have left not a name ; or some solitary mourner with Rizpah-like grief lives to guard their memory. Voices that sung God's praises are hushed in silence. Those who walked to the house of God in company are resting together in the narrow house ; and fathers and brethren and fellow partners in the journey, whom we have loved as our own soul, "have been led captive of him who opens not the house of his prisoners." What hearts have been rent in these partings that bleed afresh as memory touches the wound, and that shall never be fully healed, till the great day when the grave shall hear the word *Restore* ! As the saviour stood before the sepulchre of Lazarus, it is said with touching simplicity, "Jesus wept," and wherefore ? It was not. as John Howe has observed, over that one grave : " For he knew his own purpose and foresaw the certain and glorious case of this dark dispensation. No, but in that single death he saw many. In the weeping mourners around his eye beheld all the woe and desolation which sin and death had brought into this fair world; and then that large heart of his was melted—" he groaned in the spirit and was troubled." This one recent grave may so lead us back to many a mouldering heap around it.

> "The air is full of farewells to the dying
> And mournings for the dead."

We have been like the apostle "in deaths oft." It is not forbidden to call up the forms of the departed, although like Samuel to the unhappy king of Israel they came to tell us that we must soon be with them. The sorrow is salutary

> · O, let the soul her slumbers break,
> And thought be quickened and awake:
>   Awake to see
> How soon this life is gone and past;
> How death comes softly stealing on,
>   How silently.
>
> Our lives are rivers gliding free
> To that unfathomed boundless sea,
>   The silent grave,
> Thither all earthly pomp and boast
> Roll, to be swallowed up and lost
>   In one dark wave."

ERRATA.

Page 4, Date of the letter near the foot of the page, for "1857" read "1807."
" 6, line 10, for "2 Cor. X. 18" read 2 Cor. V. 18.
" 13, " 5, for Acts 17. 3-10. read Acts 17-31.
" " " 24, for "affecting" read "resulting."
" 18, " 9, omit "the first."
" 22, " 1, for "supplied" read "supported."
" 23, " 2, for "1829" read "1826."
" 24, " 20, for "year" read "years."